Drawn and Quartered

Fiona Murray

abuddhapress@yahoo.com

ISBN: 9798395278739

Fiona McKay 2023

®™©

Alien Buddha Press 2023

For Declan and Jane – thank you

And to all the women in my life – these stories are for you

The medieval penalty of quartering was sometimes achieved by tying each limb of the traitor to a horse and spurring them off in different directions. They say women were burned instead, dead of the smoke before the flames had licked their bodies clean. But women have always known what it is like to be pulled apart.

Love

Friendship

Family

Work

Caregiving

Self

All of these things tear women apart, from the inside out.

Contents

1 ~ Love

2 ~ Friendship

3 ~ Family

The Woman Consumed

ACure for the Linear Theory of Time

The Night Watch

Customer Service

Mother, Missing

The Magic Hour*

4 ~ Work

How to Paint a Masterpiece (In Seven Easy Steps)*

Grift*

How to Win in the Workplace – A Boardgame for Women

Trust Fall*

The Pay is Crap but the Tips are Okay

5 ~ Caregiving

Afterlife*

A Woman, a Chair, a Television, a Book, a Visitor

Mommy Dearest

The Final Stop

Visiting Time*

End Stages

6 ~ Self

A Recipe for Disaster*

All the Ways to Get Clean

Written in Ink

Leaving Home

A Temporal Haunting*

* Indicates Previously Published

1 ~ Love

Unusual Noises at Night Must Be Investigated

The ticking bomb turned out to be your watch on the nightstand.

The shrill alarm was just the telephone.

The loud retort was not a shot, but the front door slamming.

A taxi, gunning its engine down the empty road, broke the dawn.

I get out of bed and make my rounds to take stock. Your watch is gone, strapped around your wrist; your phone, in its pocket next to your heart; the wardrobe, empty except for a hanger's tinny clang.

The shattering glass is my heart.

How to Make a Gingerbread House

Ingredients:

One Mother

Three children

One Father

Method:

Add the mother and children together. Place in a one-bedroom flat over the chip-shop and leave to chill. Sift through the past, keeping aside any minor transgressions. You will need these later. Poke old tender spots until they yield disharmony.

Weigh up your chances of getting away with it, then whisk your grievances into a conversation with him to see if his opinion is as firm as it appears. If it is, he will then take out the transgressions from earlier and use them to soften your resistance. Stir up some trouble and leave to set.

Return to the family home, where he beats the children until they are stiff. At this point, if it curdles, you may have to throw everything away and start again, with fresh ingredients.

Add the mother and children together.

The Destroying Angel

I walked the foggy woods early, the moisture making pearls on every spider web that stretches across the shrubby undergrowth and anchors foliage to the ground. You didn't know I'd left the cottage. I didn't ask if I could go.

It was the perfect time for mushroom picking in the damp and coldly-humid air with its suspension of early-morning scents: rotting leaves, growth, and decay. You went out later with your basket. I took care, so you wouldn't know you weren't the first to pick today.

I hadn't understood, until I found your book, how a mushroom is just the flower of the sentient mycelium that lives underground and pushes its fingers through the crust of soil. And yet, you like to eat the things. You ridicule me because I won't.

Our ancient kitchen has an earthy smell – cold limestone underfoot, wooden shelves set into the faded red-brick walls holding my cookery books and your treasured mushroom-hunting tome. It's open to the page on Amanita. So many different types. So easy to get confused. I pick the book up in my oven-gloved hand and replace it on the shelf.

I've been paying close attention. I have nothing else to do now, since I left my family, my friends, my life. Since I swapped working, and earning, and living – for a cottage too far from a town, too close to the woods. I can't have another conversation about permission, about what I'm allowed to do. You slam the back door and drop your basket on the table.

If only you'd let me keep my phone, I could call an ambulance.

Everyone will know it was an accident. I'll be so distraught. I slide cold butter into the hot cast-iron pan your grandmother left you.

It won't be long now.

Because We Were All Young Once,
and Thought We Knew What We Wanted

I'm so lucky to live here. Everyone says so. To have found a life, and a love, in such a wholesome place. So healthy, everyone says.

Endless mud-filled green fields. Fresh air undercut with cow dung. The slow, rolling stares in the village when I pass by. I know they're scrutinising my face for the latest damage.

I pick a quiet time to catch the bus. It takes me in the wrong direction. A feint, a sleight of hand to smudge my trail. Another bus, a train; the city lights.

The hostel isn't much, but it's a beginning. I'm safe.

Ground Truth

The hail is coming down the size of unripe grapefruit, smashing into the roof of the van like mortars. The windscreen has shattered in one corner, but we can still see out. The road is empty, strewn with irregular white orbs that make it look as if the gods have been having a snowball fight, and don't know their strength. Our instruments are telling us that the centre of the storm is close, and Greg wants to know if we go into it, or retreat and limp off to get the van fixed.

You've never liked that I worked with a man, with Greg, despite the fact that he and I make a wonderful team, and our meteorological specialties complement each other. You're always suspicious of any time we spend together outside the university, calling us 'storm chasers', and not letting me explain to you the necessity of obtaining ground truth in our work: data from the field, not just other people's studies. I've tried to explain the science to you: tried to convey to you my love for this field of study, shown you photographs of fist-sized hailstones striped with clear and cloudy ice, explained to you the reasons, the fast or slow speed of the freezing water leading to those outcomes, I've drawn you diagrams, showing you how a hailstone is like a pearl, starting small and then accumulating layers, and, though not fished for, falling gracefully or spitefully to earth once the thunderstorm can no longer hold it up.

You don't listen. You don't care. To me, those are the same thing. The hours I've spent, listening to you talk about your poets, the books I've read to keep up with your work. I've been sympathetic when your applications for tenure went unrewarded. I've taken my own good news and buried it deep where it won't upset you. Those times at drinks parties, when people have drifted over to congratulate me on my professorship, I've swerved away, embarrassed by my success standing next to your perceived failure, or stood my ground, mutely begging with my eyes 'don't mention it, don't mention it, don't mention it.'

And don't get me started on our endless rows about kids. You don't think kids should have a working mother – it's like we're still in the 1950s and everything is sweet like apple-pie. The years tick by while you invent excuses: the time will be right when you're head of department, or I've found a safer line of work. That time will never come.

I think about yesterday: your side of the bed not slept in, the note on the kitchen counter, our never-born children drifting further away. Now I'm nobody's wife, nobody's mother; I have this chance in front of me and I'm not sitting on the fence any longer, worrying about what you think. I'm all in. I look into the eye of the storm. I look at Greg's exhilarated face. And I say 'Drive!'.

Iced Out

You can't breathe, and the realisation that cold can do this to you is simultaneously interesting and terrifying. The captain of the boat must notice your look of terror and calls to you to pull up your face coverings, and you pull the thin snood pooled around your neck up over your head, covering your mouth and nose, amazed at the ability of the fine fabric to cut out that bitter weather like a door closing. You're so thankful for it and finally forgiving of its ridiculous cost that had left you gasping in the specialist supply store with your list of necessary equipment.

It will take some time for these new rituals to bed in. At home, it was wallet, phone, keys. Here, it will be a spreadsheet of different layers for different activities. There are many new things to acclimatise to.

Looking out over the sound as the boat is unloaded, you pause to wonder at your life choices, and whether it was necessary to accept this posting, half a world away from anywhere, to get over things. Your ex had thought you ridiculous, but then, nothing new in that. Greg had been disappointed, as you handed over your class notes, and lecture plans to him, the deep blue of his eyes offering something you know you're not ready for. You'd kept saying that six months was so short, would go by so quickly; you hadn't known which of you this was meant to reassure.

The snow is beautiful, and blinding, and terrifying. You can easily imagine getting lost – setting out so confidently, then very soon losing your bearings and twisting around in a panic, white in every direction, formless, featureless. It scares you because that's how you feel inside right now. That's why you're here – to step away and find your lost self, wherever you are.

The men have unloaded the boat, and you watch it pull out into the water, plaiting the water in its wake into a cord you could reach out and grab hold of, pull yourself back to safety, back to where you once were. But you know that place is no longer there; that you have to build yourself a new foothold, clamber carefully to a place of safety. You stamp your feet and a surprised penguin dives aerodynamically into the water. You turn for the tiny building that will house you for half a year, and go inside to make it home.

2 ~ Friendship

The Arc of Friendship is Long and Tends Towards Gossip

Just as we arrived, as my hand was preparing to stretch out towards the buzzer, the message already leaving my brain and spiralling through my synapses, you intercepted it, placed your hand on my arm to stop me, saying 'I can't', pulling me away towards the Starbucks on the corner where we sat on a busy Saturday afternoon, huddled over our uneaten biscotti and our cooling coffee, a bubble around us; a forcefield so strong that no-one even hovered nearby and hoped to speed us up, snag our table. Tears will do that. They slide down your face and repel all invaders. You hold your cup with two hands, clinging to its vanishing warmth, and still, you say nothing. I wait, giving you the time you clearly need.

We go way back, the three of us. Well, four of us, but Alison moved so far away – Australia – that it's like she died. Every time any one of us thinks to call her, it's the middle of the night. It must always be the middle of the night in Australia, I sometimes think. So now it's you, and me, and Carrie, and we spend a lot of time playing phone tag and saying, 'let's do lunch!' like we mean it, and of course we don't, because our new lives are consuming us, eating us whole and spitting out the pips. Work is exhausting, as we swing ourselves up our various corporate ladders, or not, and we don't live near each other, criss-crossing the city on buses and tubes, never enough time for things we want, or say we want, but don't. We miss each other's news more than we miss each other's company, it seems.

But we keep up, somehow, with the gossip. It's like a gas, expanding and condensing to fit every space in our lives. That guy Carrie mentioned in passing, I hear she's dating him long before I manage to meet up with her and hear her breathless tale of love, see her eyes mist and sparkle with a happiness that can't be faked. I hear you've broken up with someone, and wait for you to tell me, and wait, and wait. I say nothing. I have make-ups and break-ups myself, and sometimes, they're not something to talk about. There's been something about you recently, though, that I can't put my finger on. A furtive kind of excitement. You'll tell me, when the time is right.

Eventually I ask why we are sitting here in a coffee chain we both hate, not drinking our coffee, instead of eating cupcakes and drinking prosecco with Carrie and her bridesmaids. I'm fairly sure you're not this upset about not having been chosen as one of them. I know I'm not. Eventually, your words spill out like rain. Those threads I dropped are stitched together again. It was him and you, then him and her. What she doesn't know: then it was him and you again, as well as him and her. You thought he'd leave her, in the end. You thought he'd choose you. He chose both, though only two of you knew. And now, you don't know how to tell him your latest news, now that you've heard his, and hers. You can't stomach coffee now, you tell me, pushing it away. You can't stomach other people's happiness and lies either.

I gently take your gift, wrapped in horseshoes and bells, put you in an extravagant taxi. I'll go without you, and see what information I can find out, at your lover's fiancée's bridal shower.

Beauty and the Beast

New Year's Eve

You are so, so beautiful. There's no chance you will ever look at me, until you do, holding my gaze until I look away, my face reddening in the humid bar. It's been raining outside, and the floor is damp from the many pairs of shoes tracking in water. I watch them. Heels, jewelled flats, brogues, trainers – yours – as you walk across the crowded space to where I'm standing. There's no way someone like you will talk to someone like me, but here you are.

Valentine's Day

These roses are so, so beautiful. Everyone in the office has stopped by to admire them, sniff them –though hot-house roses have no scent – and tell me how lucky I am. As if I didn't know. I'm excited for tonight and I want it to be perfect. The restaurant you've picked is so romantic. I'm so glad you suggested this dress – the one I bought is not nearly as flattering. Like you, your taste is exquisite.

Easter

My family is a little disappointed that we can't visit, but they're excited to hear we're engaged. They can't wait to meet you. I was hoping to have a party with some friends, or maybe a night out with the girls to celebrate. I'm so, so sorry if that makes you feel less than, if it makes you feel not enough, if it makes you feel unloved. Of course I'll stay home. I just love how you can be so vulnerable with me.

Midsummer Night

I'm so, so sorry I got it wrong. You'd been so helpful, going through my wardrobe with me, telling me what suits and what doesn't, and you're right, it is much easier to get ready in the morning with fewer things to pick from. I didn't realise that this red dress was inappropriate for going out with your friends. I can see now that I should have chosen something less noticeable, drawn less attention to myself. I know you're sorry too. I know you'll never do that again.

Halloween

I'm so embarrassed, sitting here in A&E with the drunks tearing the place apart. The triage nurse thought I was in costume, thought it was fake blood. Who are you meant to be, she asked me. I had no answer, have no answer. Have you?

Christmas

I am so glad now, that you don't have my new address; that you never took the time to know my friends. It's a shared house, and I think they've set up a rota between them. There's always someone to walk to work with me, someone just passing my new office when it's time to leave. I'm never on my own. And I'm so grateful to them for that. I'm so grateful to them for not believing me when I told them everything was fine.

We Girls

We scarper from the school gates, me and you, soluble with weekday giggles, too old for this, we tell each other, far, far too grown up. We bitch over coffee in our favourite café downtown, the one our husbands call 'The Fleece', we bitch in each other's kitchens, our ears cocked like cats to be sure the kids can't hear us gossiping, we bitch on moms' nights out, our foreheads touching as we lean in over our happy-hour watered-down cosmopolitans, our feet aching in unfamiliar heels. We embarrass our kids, shriek-singing 'Let It Go' into the wind on winter beach walks. We love to sing.

We egg each other on when the school asks for volunteers for the PTA. We text each other jokes, in those endless meetings, trying not to laugh out loud. We talk seriously about the school raffle, then explode out of meeting rooms, running, racing to get someplace where we can decompress, let it out, laugh till our stomach muscles get the best workout of our lives. We still burp with laughter days, weeks, months later when one of us says bunting, or ticket stubs, or spot prize. We work these secret code-words into normal conversations. We love these private jokes.

We might feel wistful, sometimes, on the outside of things, but these cliques are not for us. We have each other, all for one. We love to shake it off.

We thrill to the scandal when the Chairperson of the PTA resigns. We cluster hop at the school gates, swimming in the tide of news, sucking in gossip like krill, texting each other all through the dreary homework hours. Did you hear, we say. Omg, we message each other urgently, screenshotting class WhatsApp threads, our fingers flying while we make dinner, do bath night, tuck in our kids, watch tv with our husbands. The details trickle through our phones – the child, the bullying, the suspension, the PTA Chair seen in tears in the school office. What? we say, to our kids, our spouses, when they interrupt our written conversations. We love to be epistolary.

And then you message me your news. They asked you to take over the PTA. A compromise candidate between the groups. A fresh face. New blood. I reply with my favourite gif, that woman in the seafoam top, spit-laughing her coffee all over the table. The very idea. Your ellipses quiver, you are typing, then you stop. I get distracted as I pace the white lines of the football pitch, raising ragged cheers. My phone pings as I drive home to bath muddy children. When I get to check, you're telling me it's not a joke. You'd love to be useful, you say.

Now, I hop from group to group at the school gates; skating around the edges. Sometimes you're there. Sometimes, you even have a clipboard. Always, you're surrounded. And too busy for coffees, walks, and texts. I still go to the PTA meetings, to talk about the raffles, the bake sale, the Christmas Fayre. I try dropping 'bunting' into conversation, and you smile politely, say how great it would be if I would take that on. You love to rule, it seems.

Plain Sailing

It's kind of cool, the way the boat has sliced through the water, skimming out to sea. The day is deceptive, though. The sun was blinding where it danced off the water, and the 'slight breeze', as Rachel called it, was cutting through me like I was paper. And I had expected the horizon to be sharper, like a blade, not a fuzzy grey that looked like it was closing in on us.

I turn my head to see how far out we are, but someone has stolen the harbour, stolen the entire coastline, left a fuzzy strip of cottonwool in its place. And then I look back to the horizon, but the thief has been there too. The thief has taken Rachel, the boat, my hands: everything. I go to stand, and Rachel shouts at me to sit, to be still, to do what she tells me. What the hell, I say, what is this? Sea-mist, she replies. Comes surging in. I can hear the gulls, cawing their angry shriek, but muffled, the sound deadened, like they are some distance away.

This is not what I signed up for, I tell Rachel, and she snaps back that I said I'd been sailing before. And I have been, but it wasn't like this. I had sipped gin-and-tonic in a bikini, the sun all over my body like a lover, the sea breeze a cool kiss. I had not had to haul ropes that burned my palms; I had not been shouted at for my incompetence, over and over. I could be sipping a drink now, instead of this. Some great idea my daughter had: join the sailing club, mum, maybe you'll meet some new people. Just because her father has moved on.

Rachel gives me a bell, looming out of the nothingness as the boat rocks beneath her movement. I am to ring it once every minute. Long, short, long. Its puny tinkle is swallowed by the damp. I simultaneously have to hold a rope, while Rachel crawls around. She asks me if I can see the lights she's switched on. I bend over the side but I can't even see the boat. Dizziness spirals through me, and I don't know if I'm still leaning out over the water or if I've sat up again. I tell Rachel I'm going to be sick; she tells me to pull myself together. She is hauling the sails up like a venetian blind; I hear the slither of the fabric, the thwack of the ropes. We have to anchor, she tells me, and we do, the chain clacking down into the water. Once we're no longer moving, the cold has its way with me, its fingers everywhere. I can feel my teeth shivering against each other, chattering.

I ask Rachel if we should ring the coastguard and she swears, quietly. For fuck's sake, she whistles through her teeth, we're not in any danger, so we won't waste their time. Ring the fucking bell again. The whole point is to make ourselves known, avoid a collision. The mist will lift, eventually, she tells me. She is so competent, Rachel. Her husband didn't leave her; he died, but that's different, that's not intentional. I breathe in the smell of sea and salt and decay, let the breath out again, repeat. My skittering heart begins to settle.

I think we might talk. I think this might be a thing that draws us together. I picture us in one of the bars along the harbour, over cocktails with other women our age, children flown, taking up new hobbies. I picture us telling this story, how the first time we hung out together, we end up stranded in fog in the middle of the ocean. I picture Rachel leaning in to correct me: sea-mist, sea. I try to tell Rachel this, but she tells me to shut up and ring the fucking bell again, am I timing it, there are rules, once per minute, had I not heard her? Short, long, short. She is busy listening, she said. I listen too. I hear the slide of wave over wave, I hear my own breathing, I hear the silence as our nascent friendship dies on the deck between us, and we wait, and we wait, and we wait for the wind to rise and clear the skies again.

Generous Donations

'And do you know what I said to her then?' Carol asks, which means she pauses for a nano-second before continuing, 'I said to her, what you need to do is let him fend for himself for a while. Kick him out, change the locks, let him stew. That told her.'

I'll bet it did, and I feel sorry for Carol's friend, if the only person she can confide in is Carol, and I say *but isn't she the one whose son has just started college*, and Carol jumps in before I finish my sentence. 'Yes,' she says, 'a big lump of eighteen, he should be out earning a living instead of partying and asking her for money,' and I think *is that what his crime was? Being a student, basically?* But I say nothing because she's probably told me before, and I kind of zone out when she starts one of her stories.

I wheel over the big blue skip – where people can dump their bags of donations – and pull on my rubber gloves. I've learned not to plunge my hands into a bag of donations – who donates broken china, you might wonder – and instead I spread it out on the floor, kneeling to sort

41

through the rubble of people's lives. You can learn a lot from what's given away. We got an engagement ring once, which made me sad. Not sad that the marriage had broken up – so many do – just sad I'd never had a ring like that.

Carol doesn't kneel. 'I can't be getting down on the floor with my arthritis,' she's always saying, and it's fine, I'll get through it faster on my own, sorting the things we can sell from the dross.

Black, patent high heels. Nice. I hand them up to Carol, who puts a date sticker on the sole, prices them up.

'In my day,' she continues, 'Young people had a bit of respect for their parents.'

In your day, I say in my head, *dinosaurs roamed the earth*. I shake out a black mini dress, slashed to the hip at either side.

'That's disgracefully short,' Carol comments, pulling it out of my hands. 'Still, I suppose some young one will buy it. I hope you never let your daughter wear anything like this, so short and so tight. What is the fabric, do you think?'

Rubber, is what I think, and I'm not likely to let my daughter wear it, not even on Halloween. Carol won't remember Mollie is only five, only just started school. Carol claims it's too hard to tell us 'young ones'

apart and remember our details. That we're not here long enough

before we move on. Six months we're here, as part of the back-to-work

scheme. Six months on our tiny allowance, then hopefully a real job, if

I can make it work with Mollie in school. Carol doesn't 'have to be

doing this' she's always reminding us, like some kind of blessing.

Something silver glitters on the floor, and I pick up a strip of leather

and studs.

'That's a very large dog collar,' Carol says, 'but it can go in the

window display with the pet items.'

Oh, I wouldn't put that with pet items, I think but don't say as Carol

hustles off. She's obsessed with stuff for dogs – little bandanas for

them to wear, jewelled collars for her 'babies', novelty jumpers. You

should see her Facebook page. The dogs look just mortified in her

photos. I pick up more leather, studs, chains, as Carol returns to take it

from my protesting hands.

'Trying to keep that one for yourself? You don't even have a dog. And

you know our policy, no purchases by the staff before the items go into

the shop.' She tsks under her breath, and that's the moment I decide to say nothing. Sure, I think, as we wrestle bondage dresses onto our two 'lady-mannequins' as Carol calls them, sure, as we line up the six-inch heels, sure, as she lays out sex-harnesses in the pet section.

I'll take a photo of the window display for the social media, I tell Carol. Elaborating, *the Facebook page*, when she looks mystified. I know the effect this will have.

'No, I'll do that myself,' she says, and off she goes. I go back to sorting donations in the back, and I try not to laugh. I had been glad to get this work placement, thought it would be good to get out, meet people, make new friends. Maybe the next placement will be better and while I'm here, I'll get what enjoyment out of it I can.

3 ~ Family

Woman Consumed

Her teeth were the first to go: calcium leeched out by the hungry succubus howling silently in the skyless sea. Then her hair: great drifts in the shower to accompany the swelling.

Then he left, and she healed over his absence like a blister, cushioning herself against the loss. The splinter remained, underneath. A project started together must be finished alone. She continues on. She will always keep going.

The last thing is her flesh: her body yielding up every ounce, every fragment tucked between organs or under her skin. Pulled, all pulled through the glorious machine of her carcass, through the slackened breasts, pulled through by the desperate hunger, turning the mother herself into milk.

A Cure for the Linear Theory of Time

'Play with me, play with me,' he tugs at you.

Sneaking a glance at the clock, you ask 'What have I been doing all

morning?' Remembering cars, lego, dinosaurs.

'But I'm bored! I want to play the yes-no game.'

You look at your coffee cooling on the table, give in with bad grace – a

sigh you try to hide.

'Ok, I'll play for five minutes, how's that? How do we play?'

'I ask you a question, but you have to answer without saying yes or no.'

You think it sounds like hell, give him an extra squeeze to compensate.

'What's your favourite colour, mommy?'

You think of all your favourite things: coffee, reading without

interruption, travel.

'Blue,' you answer.

'Blue's not your favourite colour, It's my favourite colour, mommy,

not yours!'

'Yes it is,' you insist. The blue sea of the Mediterranean, cloudless skies, the unbroken water of an empty swimming pool. A moment that is shattered by laughter.

'You're out, you're out, you said YES!' He is laughing and crowing and pointing.

Anger rises through you and lifts your hand. You must not shout, must not hate this triumphant jeering, must not hit. Instead, you let your hand fall to your hair and tuck it back. Instead, you breathe, deep and long.

'I'm out,' you say, 'so it's my turn to ask the questions?'

'Yes, you now.'

You resist an easy win, and look around, as if for inspiration but really seeking out the clock's arthritic hands.

'I guess I'll have to ask – is Danger Mouse your favourite TV programme?'

He pauses, searching out your trap.

'It is,' he says carefully, 'it is my favourite. Can I watch it now?'

'Yes,' you say, thinking of your coffee, your phone in your pocket, and silence.

The Night Watch

39C

You're in our bed, hot, burning up, pushing off the heavy winter duvet.
You're here so I can keep watch through the night, keep taking your
temperature, keep giving you doses of the medicines, liquid spoons of
sweetness that will drive your fever down, down, down. Won't they? I
insert the thermometer carefully in your ear, press the button, wait for
the night-loud beep to find out the answer. It is the time before my
phone comes with a torch, so I struggle to read the digits in the dark.
Your eyes are open, and you stare at something I can't see, pointing
your little finger in the dark. The fairies are so beautiful, you tell me,
look, they're glowing like stars. Hush, my darling I tell you. This will
not kill you, I promise, silently.

38C

I'm so proud of you, darling, you're doing so well, I say, as you throw
up again, vomit neatly caught in a plastic bowl. The first time, you
weren't so lucky, and I'm holding you on my lap, a bit too big for that
now, but you need the comfort of my body, while we change the sheets,

air the room, clean, clean, clean with disinfectant. It's a bug – she has a fever, I say, reading off the display in the bright bedroom light. Inwardly, I feel my body shudder. If you have that stomach bug, it's likely tomorrow I will have it too. We won't die from this, I think.

37.5C

You're not sick, I say, though you look it: face pale, eyes bright but red from tears. It all came pouring out after midnight, when I ached to lie down, and you ached to talk. The evening confessions, I've always called it, when the things you've managed to push down all day come bubbling to the surface in the silence of your room. I'll write a note for school tomorrow, I offer, bringing you a cup of camomile tea to rehydrate you after your tears. Friendships break, mend; sometimes stronger. But love always leaves you open to pain, pain, pain. I remember this feeling, I tell you; you think life can't go on, but it will.

37C

I sit at the table in the kitchen sipping coffee too late into the night. You hate when I do this; wait up till you're home. I tell you I'm reading or watching tv. That I didn't feel sleepy, had work to catch up on, a book to read. All true, in their way, just not as urgent as I suggest. The clock on the wall is a midnight metronome. I'm almost nodding to the beat, my head moving in time. You're an adult, you're my child, adult, child, adult, child. I have to let you go, live your life, go on dates with strangers, drink in bars. It won't kill you, my darling, will it?

Customer Service

Your wait time is approximately 37 minutes

You stand in the kitchen, leaning against the fridge, with your mobile held to your ear. Listening to the words, a surge of anger boils through you, like a tidal wave in a tank: fury contained in a small space, with no possibility of release. Unless the tank shatters. You are that tank.

Your wait time is approximately 31 minutes

It isn't as though you are even doing this for yourself. You try to shut out the glitchy music and the irregular announcements that get your hopes up for a moment, and then drop you back into your emotional stew: they're just another recording. You are trapped in a loop.

Your wait time is approximately 29 minutes

If only you could use this time for something else. You balance the phone in a way that will cause the physio to tut over the knot in your neck and start cleaning down the worktops and filling the dishwasher one-handed. Now you're doing two things you hate. Is that better, or worse, you ask yourself. You have no answers.

Your wait time is approximately 19 minutes

The kitchen now looks clean and tidy. You look at your watch in surprise, thinking that more time must surely have passed. If things can look tidy this quickly, why don't you do this more often? You check yourself. This chore isn't hard, so why is it yours? You know why – if you're not doing it, you're managing it. You're so damn tired of managing.

Your wait time is approximately 17 minutes

You ruminate on all the lost minutes in your life: minutes like these where you are waiting, waiting, waiting to do something for someone else. You wish you could herd them all together into a file marked 'time' and spend them as you need them. Thinking of spending pings a memory. You flip through a stack of mail and pull out the bills.

Your wait time is approximately 13 minutes

You walk the house in circles, picking things up and putting them away, composing sentences in your brain that will be the key to getting everyone to do this for themselves; to keep the place the way they like it, without it falling to you. You hit on just the right combination of words, and you will write it down once you've put these dirty clothes in the hamper and brought these plates to the sink. You forget the magic formula as soon as you pick up the pen.

Your wait time is approximately 7 minutes

You picture your life: a fast-forward of motion, of picking up and putting away, of cooking and cleaning, of doing and dusting; you at the centre of the frame, ageing and wrinkling like that one apple left in the bowl. You should clean out that bowl.

Your wait time is approximately 3 minutes

With deliberate intent, you press the red button, ending the call.

Mother, Missing

The woman pictured on the milk carton isn't Janna. The woman pictured on the side of the milk carton in her hand isn't her, but it could be. Janna can picture exactly the moment when the woman leaves her house.

***

The final straw is milk, ironically. The woman had been getting the kids up that morning, negotiating them into their hated uniforms, standing over them as they brush their teeth and go downstairs to find their missing shoes and sports kit. She had even promised them that cereal they liked, with the chocolate coating, though it tasted to her like earth and dust.

The previous evening, the woman had noticed they were getting low on milk, shaking the carton speculatively. She had been making dinner.

The beef thing. Cubes of dripping, bloody flesh browned in batches. Time consuming, for a Tuesday, but mum, mum, please make that, it's our favourite. Slice, chop, dice, stir, open the fridge, shake, distractedly. Mike, she had called out into the yawning house, Mike, can you get some milk, we're nearly out. Yeah, Cass, sure. After I've gone for a run. After dinner. Later. After.

Wednesday morning, the carton, is empty, as is the coffee cup beside the dishwasher. Beside it, not in it. The shower is running, and she grabs her car keys. I'm just going for the milk, she calls up the stairs. The milk, not just any milk. The milk you finished. The milk you were going to get yesterday. The endless emotional load of damn milk.

The woman lets the door slam a little, and a neighbour's CCTV catches her driving past at 7.45am. The security cameras in the local Spar show grainy images of a dark-haired woman moving through the store, putting items in a wire basket, stopping at the fridge, taking down a carton of milk. Staring at it. Staring, then slowly putting it back and walking out of the store.

Janna knows what happens next. The woman drives for a long time, but not back to the house where Mike is finally out of the shower, texting: Cassie, Where u? – no reply – Cass?, Cass, why aren't you answering your phone? He's making light of things in the kitchen, playing fun dad, dealing with the fallout when he realises there's no milk for the cereal, making toast instead, his cheer wearing thin when the kids complain their toast is too dark, too light, not enough butter, too much. Cassie? I'm leaving in 10 minutes whether you're back or not. But he doesn't, because she isn't.

The roads stretch out, unspooling endlessly across the dry countryside. The woman can see harvesters at work from the motorway, chopping and shucking. She stops at a service station and takes out a lot of cash, Mike will later find out, and she's captured as a tiny figure filling the car with petrol, driving off. The motorway gives way to smaller roads and the trail runs cold – no tolls or cameras to log her progress.

Mike doesn't report that she's gone for some time. First, he assumes she's coming back, probably with the milk the kids say she went to buy. When she doesn't, he phones in sick to work, gets the kids to school.

When she's not back that evening, he reluctantly phones her mother, not wanting to have to even ask if she's there, but she's not. Must be staying with a friend, he says. What he doesn't say – to punish me for not buying the fucking milk. He's angry now, but still plays fun dad with the kids. As if she's watching, as if she can see him thinking: See, see how easy this is! But he's exhausted.

When the motorway runs out, and the good road with the hard shoulder fades into one where two cars can pass, just, and the light begins to fade, she stops at a pub where the barmaid is also the waitress, and run off her feet. Cassie orders the lasagne with chips, not caring how bad it will be. Maybe it's having someone to hand it to her, then take away the plate and clean it, but it's the best thing she has ever eaten. When things quieten down, she tells the waitress she's on a driving holiday, asks if there's anywhere to stay. The waitress kindly doesn't ask where her bags are, when she shows her to an upstairs room rarely let out. Doesn't ask her why she's chosen this backwater for a holiday. Takes the money and lets her be. Serves her breakfast in the morning, heaping her plate with toast. Tells her they're hiring, if she's interested, so she parks her car around the back where it can't be seen, puts on an apron and gets to work.

Her phone dies, and she lets it, leaving it uncharged in her bag. Still, she's surprised how long it takes before she sees Mike on TV, doing the whole missing person press conference. The pub is busy, and nobody's watching the news. Nobody is putting it all together, and she doesn't pay the TV any attention, busy with carrying hot plates, collecting plates, refilling the milk jugs on the tables.

At night though, she thinks of her children, and the pain in her chest, in the back of her throat where tears start, won't go away. She's falling, falling, like in an avalanche, trying to hold onto things that are also falling. She can't stay. She can't go back. She can't stay away. The pain, the pain of missing them.

***

The woman pictured on the milk carton isn't Janna. The woman pictured on the side of the milk carton in her hand isn't her, but sometimes she wishes it was. Janna puts the carton back on the shelf, leaves her basket on the floor, and walks out of the store.

The Magic Hour

The sun is shining relentlessly as I chase my two across the sand for what must be the millionth time today. Exit, pursued by a mother with sunscreen, I think. I don't laugh though, as I'm a little out of breath and in a hurry. Why must my kids be the ones to do full-body exfoliation with sand, as though this were a fancy spa and not the local beach heaving with people on an unexpectedly sunny bank holiday weekend? And while it may be a tiny bit funny, my kids have some red-hair genes buried deep in their DNA, so multiple applications of factor 50 are required on the rare occasions that the sun shines, and more are needed when they keep scrubbing the damn stuff off with sand.

I'm on the long sandy beach that they argued for this morning, where the tide is shallow and has retreated leaving some sandbars and puddles packed with kids playing. I can't see mine anywhere, and they were right there a second ago. I feel panic begin to rise and imagine the headlines: 'Useless Mother Loses Not One But TWO Children On Day

Out', 'Danger Lurks on Sunny Beach', 'Search for Missing Twins Goes Into Second Day'.

I catch a flicker of red and, quickly turning my head, I see my pair rounding the point separating this boring stretch of flat sand – 'but it's so good for making sandcastles, Mommy!' – from my favourite beach, the one with rocks and coves and gritty sand, fewer ice cream vans and deeper water.

I give chase and round the point a moment later, a bit disorientated, if I'm honest, after sitting in the sun. It's hotter than I imagined here, where there's no breeze and the sun dazzles and shimmers like a curtain of light. I pass through and a waiter approaches with a tray of cocktails, motioning me to a waterside table. I place my jewelled bag on the table and wonder where the sunscreen went. The silk of my kaftan pools around me as I sit, and I know for sure that I wasn't wearing this earlier as I don't own anything made of silk or that pools in elegant folds – not anymore, and never this nice. I take the cocktail and look around me. Couples and small groups are at the other tables, the sun is beginning to set, and there is a scent of flowers, growing herbs, and salt. I sip my drink and see the waiter approach with plates of food. He is followed by someone who has a smile that would rival the dazzle of the sun, hurrying towards my table. I stand up to greet him and am dazzled again by the setting sun. I shield my eyes and take a step.

'Excuse me! Hello? Are these your children?'

I'm gazing down the length of the sandy beach and a young lifeguard has my kids by the hand.

'They were heading out too far and the tide is turning.'

I take their hands and pull them wordlessly back to our picnic blanket where I cover them with sunscreen and pass around sandwiches with my sticky hands while the sun winks off a plastic gemstone nestling on the rug.

4 ~ Work

How to Paint a Masterpiece (In Seven Easy Steps)

You will need:

Paper

Canvas

Charcoal sticks

Pencils (HB, 2HB, 4HB)

Eraser

Oil paints

Linseed oil

Variety of brushes

Turpentine (for cleaning and erasure)

1. Prep your canvas. Tell it what to expect. Expect greatness, you tell it.

2. Use your pencils and paper to make a preparatory sketch. Stare at the paper, awaiting the greatness. If greatness does not come, make a cup of coffee, and let it cool while you stare out of the window at the

wonder and complexity of nature, and contemplate your inability to transfer it to paper, and your inability to be a good daughter.

3. Make some experimental marks on the canvas with charcoal. Realise they look nothing like the life you had envisaged when you were seventeen, and erase them, if possible, along with memories of the first person you ever loved, and left behind when you went away to college, and he did not, and what long-distance love would have changed about those promiscuous college years.

4. Thin down the oil paints on your palette with some linseed oil, as you have thinned down your body to fit in with the notion of the starving artist. You're always hungry, just not always for food. You're never satisfied, and that includes by food.

5. Tentatively, pick up one of your brushes, the angled one you first learned to use when you were having an affair with your painting tutor, and he used to run the sables tips of brushes over your naked body in a way that was more erotic than anything you've experienced with any lover since, though that didn't stop you from sleeping with many, many

artists, with many, many sable-tipped brushes, but it was never the same.

6. Remind yourself that Art is meant to engage, meant to provoke. Stare blankly around your suburban, three bed semi-detached house looking for an image, any image that will encapsulate all you want to say. Find that you can't put in words what you want to say, which may be part of the problem. Settle for painting a quick sketch of the dirty breakfast dishes, still on the table, the way you settled for Steve after your painting tutor moved on to a student in the year below – taller, thinner, edgier than you – whose every painting was about death.

7. Check your watch, and quickly find a smaller canvas, paint an adequate picture of a bird feeding her chick, like one you saw this morning. Paint it quickly because soon you'll have to put the paints away and hurry to do the school-run for your own chick, and your time will be over. And it won't be a masterpiece, and it's not about death, but it will probably sell at your local craft fair, because that's what people like.

Grift

Lisa yanks her dress into place, flimsy sequins winking neon-yellow, candy-pink, acid-green, walking past the yammering slots, arms ratcheting down, over and again, coins out, coins in; the house always wins. Cleavage showing, ass covered – just – a trail of silence as she passes through the bomb-loud room, explosions of music, grenades of money, hell-storm behind her like an action movie. In her head: walking through the flames.

Door says, 'Employees Only'. Everybody knows – behind here is the real action. Everything else: window-dressing. Slinks across the room and takes her place, hip-bones to the table, back arched – mirror-practised pose. Penguin-suited chick drops off her usual, rum-and-coke just so, all ice and coke, teaspoon of rum over the top. The little details. A Cuba Libre, mouthed poutily. Classy.

The regulars at the table pay no notice. Always some fresh meat though. Out-of-towners passing through. The best kind. A minor dalliance, written off, re-written before they reach home. And always,

always give a false name that they forget halfway through the evening. So many Brads and Buds.

Tonight's mark: actually called Mark – files it away in her brain to laugh over with the penguins, shoes slipped off puffy feet, out the back smoking by the stinking bins, under the kitchen vent, belching stale fat into the humid night. Later. Now is work.

Mark's in town for business, heard about the place from the concierge at his hotel, on the QT, green bills folded into palms, discreet nods. Lisa smiles. That's how it works. Chains of money. Yes, she says, she comes here sometimes, likes to watch the action, you know? It's so – pause – exciting.

Drinks keep coming. Cu-ba Li-bre. Sultry sounding, hot night, fanning herself with a cocktail napkin, drawing attention to the bead of sweat that forms, and falls, slowly, down the canyon between her perky breasts. Distracting, maybe.

Mark the mark is careful. Until he isn't. Distracted, maybe. Gets her to blow on the dice for luck. Can't believe how cheese that is, but tosses hair and blows. He buys more drinks, orders champagne, apple-bitter after the sweet Coke; she sips delicately. He slips her a few chips every time he wins. They're stashed in her purse. Some guys demand them back when their luck changes, like that's how it works. Their luck always changes.

Mark talks about his family. The sick mom, the dead dad. No rings, but responsibilities. And work – they all talk about work like it's a religion. But also about nieces and nephews, fun times, laughing faces. His own face lighting up for a family he doesn't yet have.

Later, with the penguins chattering, she's quiet. They tease, joke, prod, making her spill out her night's chips, impressed; nice bonus on top of what she's paid. But in her head, she's somewhere else: on the road, passenger seat of a nice sedan, hogging the radio, singing along, wind in her hair, new life ahead. Never fall for a mark: the first rule they'd given her.

How to Win in the Workplace – A Board Game for Women

1. Throw a six to start...

You graduate top of your class and make the rounds of interviews, surprised that you don't always get called to the second round, despite that guy – the one whose results were so far below yours – doing so. Eventually, you find a job you are happy enough with. Not perfect, but not bad.

2. Throw your hands in the air...

When you realise that the guy, the guy who always placed lower than you in college, whose degree is two whole grades lower than yours, has a job with the same firm. And is being paid more than you.

3. Throw a tantrum when...

After you have brought in the clients, after you've done all the work that was asked of you, after you stayed late so many nights that your friends joke about how you've joined witness protection – until you notice they don't joke any more, don't ask you out anymore – after all that, when that time of year comes around and the promotions and the bonuses are being handed out: they are not handed to you. The guys in the office golf society are 'seen as having management potential'.

4. Throw a sickie and...

Start interviewing around. You start to get the sense that you aren't as far along in your career as you should be, though you hadn't noticed because you've been too busy actually doing the work that your so-called career should be based on. It would appear that instead of doing your job, you should have been attending conferences and 'building your profile'. Like Gary.

5. Throw a drink in his face because...

At the conference, the kind of thing that you're supposed to be attending, where nothing useful is achieved and nothing interesting is learned and nothing valuable is discussed, Gary – how is Gary your boss now? How? – puts his hand on your ass and suggests that you could get where you want to be if you would just loosen up a little, if you know what he means, and oh yes, you know what he means because he couldn't be clearer, the creep.

6. Throw caution to the wind after...

The disciplinary hearing during which you lose your job, after 'humiliating a member of management at an industry event'. You tell them exactly what you think of them and why you would not ever recommend anyone to work with them. They remind you that anything you say along those lines would be actionable, and they escort you from the building with your belongings in a brown cardboard archive box.

7. Throw your hat in the ring at...

The many interviews you attend, where you have to be increasingly inventive in explaining why you've left your previous employment. 'Creative differences' is the best you can come up with. Finally, you get a job, and vow to spend some time on yourself.

8. Throw up when...

You see two blue lines on a stick. And you've only just started dating this guy – making a little time for your life as well as your work. When you were finally making some progress in the new job. Time to think it out again.

Trust Fall

Three-ring high, her smile nailed on with paint and practice, she is poised to dive. It has taken effort to get here. The many, many steps that have burnt her thighs as she smiles, waves, points her toes. The many, many years of practice, stripping her body down to its gears and levers; a machine capable of simulating flight. The crowd roars, the spotlight dazzles, she reaches out for the swinging bar.

Timing,

The impossible art of knowing when to arc out, when to let go. She has never thought to wonder who first had seen the potential in lengths of rope and wooden bars. The tall, tall ladders were added later. And eventually, the net. If asked, a person not conversant with this art will describe two pendula swinging wide, then close, in mathematical harmony. Not so, not so. The arcs swing out of regulation, precision drilled into the bones. And swing, and go, and swing, and higher, and swing, and release, and tumble, and catch. Or fall.

Timing,

The second spot comes on, illuminating him, his brilliant face. The crowd can't see back through time, the hours and years spent swinging, counting, catching. Can't see the sweat, the tawdry sequins. From their distance, the crowd sees only glamour. She can't see, from where she waits, the lines and creases of his frown. Can't read the map of his mood. Can only count, count, and believe.

Timing,

Looking down, she can feel the burn of the net, so many, many times. The times she fell. The times he didn't catch her. It was never clear which were errors, which were opportunities to learn. He would always tell her she must stay sharp. Never take anything for granted. Gravity would always be there, waiting, waiting to catch her out. She is always keeping watch, and it's exhausting.

Timing,

The music isn't incidental, despite how haphazard it may seem. The careful, structured beats are there, though the tune leers woozily through tinny amplification. The waves of sound disintegrate trying to reach the top of the tent. But underneath it all, they are counting, counting, counting, like a heartbeat. He grabs the bar on 'four' and gets the rhythm building.

Timing.

The drumroll is unleashed from far below them, a signal to the crowd, though not for her. Distantly, they stop their chatting. One hundred feet away, they raise their eyes. Her hands are chalked against the sweat, and ready. He's swinging through the air with arms outstretched. If ever there was a time to doubt him, his waning strength, his jealousy, his fear. She grabs the bar, steps out into air, to fly.

The Pay is Crap but the Tips are Okay

As ceremonies go it's so totally bogus that I can't believe people actually pay for it, but they do, even though we're serving up sushi and fluffy cheesecake – I mean, seriously?

Anyway, I'm sweating in my kimono even though it's the light summer one, but the city has been trapped in a glass ball of heat for ten days and each day is getting hotter with no end in sight. I'm praying for thunder and wishing I didn't have a deep, thick obi belted around my waist. In this small space, with boiling water pots and kneeling people, I feel the sweat trickle down my back and under my arms, and though my hair is put up in a formal style, it's wet to the roots and I'm in fear of the sweat washing off my pale make-up and revealing me for who I am – a total imposter frothing the matcha tea and handing around tiny plates of food.

At the beginning, when I thought this was all for real, I read up about the tea ceremony because my friend Hiroko persuaded me to tag along to the interview with her, and I was saying no way, because I'm half Italian and this is your gig, not mine, there's no way they'll want me, but turns out my waitressing experience was at least as valuable as her being actually Japanese, because this job is all about extracting money from tourists, not 'a ceremony of purity and harmony'.

Once our shift is over, we run down the steps and burst out into the humid evening, still light, still bright, still suffocatingly hotter than believable, and within minutes we're passing Leicester Square and it's teeming, heaving with more people than my mind can cope with after the quiet afternoon on the tatami mat. Tourists and Londoners – everyone is hot, wearing shorts, sandals, and there isn't a jacket to be seen in a granite city not built for heat. Guys with their shirts off are walking down the middle of the street and cars are hooting and even the police have short-sleeved shirts in this weather, and it's too much for Hiroko; she's wiped so she heads home to lie in a cold bath to recover from today and prepare for tomorrow and I keep going, cutting through the crowds in Chinatown and the lads with their oi-oi-oi as I pass. I ignore them and duck and weave through quieter streets, slowing now and enjoying the feel of a city full of purpose as the evening comes, and

I'm tossing my hair and swinging into the café like I own the place, and Giuseppe is on and he gets to work before I even order, and the sound is like gravel and water in a blender, and the smell is nearly the best part, as the dark liquid jets into the cup and he places it in front of me and I have been just dying all day for this cup of coffee.

5 ~ Caregiving

Afterlife

At night the photographs come alive. It's harder for the paintings; the paint cracks slightly with the movement, but the resulting ghosts are more deeply vivid and in technicolour.

Eleanor doesn't tell her family that she sees them, instinctively anticipating their disbelief, but makes excuses to slip down from the flat above the shop – away from all the anger of the living, to spend time with the dead.

She loves their stories, and when the opportunity arises to pass through to their world, she jumps.

Eleanor smiles so much more now. And doesn't care how much it cracks the paint.

A Woman, a Chair, a Television, a Book, a Visitor

The visitor speaks, but the woman doesn't look up.

The woman looks at the television; the visitor looks at the book.

The visitor starts to speak; the woman points at the images on the screen.

Fire and flood and earthquake rain across the screen ending the world in many ways; the visitor opens the book.

The chair rocks and shakes and moans, its wheels tracking across the lino floor; the visitor turns a page, reads out a phrase.

Inside the woman, the fires and floods and earthquakes rock and shake and moan; inside the visitor, words nudge against other words in an orderly way.

The crying woman will not be consoled; the visitor offers to turn on the television, before visiting time is over.

Mommy Dearest

You bring her a cup of tea and it's too hot and burns her mouth. You know this isn't true because you sat your meat thermometer in it for a full three minutes, checked it. But still. You know how perception of heat can be a subjective thing. She leaves the tea down for a full minute, then says it's gone cold. The laws of physics don't apply here; they're too scared to.

While you make another cup of tea – *The right temperature this time, please* – you listen to the kettle rattle, peruse the spice rack, but find nothing that you could slip in the tea to stop the flow of words, judgments. You wish the medicine cabinet was in the kitchen too. You bring in the tea, some cakes your daughter made.

Her eyes follow your hand as you take a cake, peel the yellow paper case carefully from the base, bite into the rich pink icing. Each bite is an explosion of sweetness, velvet butter, warm vanilla. You look up to see the disgusted face she makes when you eat. She pushes the cupcake around her plate, and you revel in her difficulty. *I'll save this for later, I couldn't eat another bite.* You'd call it fifteen-love but this isn't tennis, and you feel no love at play.

Tell me about your childhood, your daughter says. You freeze. You tell your therapist that you want your daughter's to be different. He's practical, asks how you plan to do this. You tell him you will allow her to feel anger, hate the world, hate you; tell him you're not afraid of your love breaking if it's stretched. You love how his face doesn't bend out of shape when you speak; how he can absorb all your words. You don't love him – you're not stupid, you know what transference is – but you love that he never gives you the silent treatment when you say difficult things. *He's paid to listen to you,* you imagine her say in your ear, *I'm the only one who'll be really honest with you.* You tell him 'What other people think of me is none of my business,' and he laughs, jots it down.

'Love can be unconditional,' you say.

You think about the time you held the pillow in your hands. You think about the time you crushed the tablets into powder. You think about the time you almost swerved the car. You phone a nursing home, make an appointment to view their rooms. You get the silent treatment. It used to give you fear. But now, you feel your power. You find silence is now just a relief.

The Final Stop

'Do you think I'll need this?' she asks, holding out an ancient, crumbling swimsuit, baggy to the touch, that I know has not been worn in twenty years.

'I don't think so,' I reply, and gently try to take it from her to put on the other pile.

'But if I need it, and I don't have it, you won't bring it over to me in time,' she says, not letting go.

I say nothing and let her put it into the suitcase we're packing, knowing I'll be repacking it once she tires of this and wanders off to sit down. I place it on top of the ski suit that isn't even hers but belonged to my sister in her younger, fitter days. They've said the thing to do is not argue about this kind of thing, to just let it go. I wouldn't have the energy anyway, though sometimes I think that's what she wants: to argue about something trivial, so she doesn't have to deal with the important things.

'He saw me across a crowded room, you know, and he had to fight his way to me, and he was so afraid that I'd be gone before he would get there,' she says, lifting up a photograph from beside the bed. It's a picture of me and my husband, on our wedding day, but I don't say that. I don't remind her that she met Dad when they worked together in the same office. There was no crowded room, but she's seen some tv movie with this trope, and now she has folded it into her history, like salt into a cake; all wrong, and leaving a bad taste in my mouth.

'He was so charming,' she croons to the photo of my husband, and I quell the urge to grab it from her and crush it into the bin under the dressing table. 'Is he meeting us there?'

I don't know how to answer this. My father is obviously not meeting us anywhere, as we have just buried him, and my ex-husband, the one she's smiling at, is hopefully as far away as it's possible to be, and still be on the same planet. Further would be better.

I don't remind her about how the paramedics had to pull him off me when he had choked me so hard I had fainted, and how she had told me

I shouldn't prosecute him, how I must have just misunderstood things. Looking back, my sister said, maybe that was early evidence of the dementia, but I'm not so sure. My sister wasn't there. She never is.

'Time to go,' I say, as I slide the unneeded items out of the suitcase and zip it up. I bring it, and her, to the car, and settle them in.

'What time will you be collecting me, to bring me home?' she asks.

'When they tell me you're ready,' I reply, knowing they never will.

Visiting Time

I take the long way round. I drive the coast road through my childhood and teenage years. When I reach the spot where I'm the one who makes the decisions, I pull over for a moment.

The wind is from the south and the sea is almost green. It has a churned quality to it.

The waves roll out; the waves roll in. I count my breaths in time to the water. I can't go on, but I do. The visiting hours are two to four. I arrive on time.

Maybe today will be a day you remember my name.

End Stages

February

St Brigid's Day, a simple cross made of soaked and shaped reeds,

celebrating spring. 'Spring,' you laugh at me, 'You're stupid to think

it's spring before the daffodils are up.' But that's to disavow the secrets

the soil is keeping; the budding, the unfurling, happening deep

underground, unseen. It starts before any colour cracks the earth.

March

St Patrick's Day. Patron saint of Irish-dancing girls whose blue-cold

legs show above poodle socks, in hail and sleet and wind. You

comment on the great show of yellow dancing heads in the verges, as I

push you, smugly wrapped up in your chair, my knuckles stinging from

the cold, to see the parade in sun, and wind, and rain.

April

Easter. You order me to swap out your winter clothes for lighter things,

also reminding me 'ne'er cast a clout till May is out', and asking where

your warm vests are. I hesitate – the long-range forecast isn't looking good – but you override me saying you've seen the news; there's a heatwave on the way. I don't correct you; there's no point in telling you the report is for a different country. I change the subject, like they've suggested would be best in these circumstances.

May

May day. You curse me for swapping out your winter clothes as the sky folds black, and spits down pellets of ice that sting. The rough weather of the cuckoos is here, that first nine days of May that vault us back to earlier months. It's not the first time we've seen this, either of us, so why am I the fool?

June

I ask if you sat out in the lovely weather we've been having. You punish me with silence. I picture you in the nursing home, face set in anger, failing to keep your temper with people you consider beneath you. Your silence is no punishment at all. I tip my face to the sun like a flower, take a sip of my wine and silently end the call.

July

I take a holiday, two weeks of exploration – art and culture and food and wine and balmy salt water and the kind of heat that warms the very centre of my bones. They tell me you've taken a fall, but not to worry, they're managing everything. Enjoy yourself, they say, you deserve it. Your view is different. I hear a note of triumph as you order me to return home. For once, I don't.

August

Death is creeping in unnoticed. Leaves are drying and curling – not from the heat as some think, but because now is autumn, mellowing into coolness at either end of the day, despite a sunny middle. You do not tell me I'm stupid to call August anything other than the summer it clearly is. You cannot tell me anything now. You have been planted deep, but next spring, you will not regrow.

6 ~ Self

A Recipe for Disaster

Ingredients:

Three kinds of sugar, slowly mixed, left to infuse, mixing, melting,

cooling, sugar, sugar, sugar.

Method:

Mix the sugar together with creamy nights and sweet days; divide

between available years.

Slide under gentle heat to bloom: growing and swelling.

Add more sugar, always more, sugar days blending into sugar nights.

Hours whisk by like speeding trains, pulling memories behind, sucking

them down like milkshake through a straw, thick and dreamy, then

gone. Hours, minutes, years, seconds, eons, nanos. Everything in equal

measure.

Beat away the family and friends that just want to help you, just want the best for you, just want, just want, just want. Ice them out. Break free of the mould they try to fit around you. You know better; you know sugar; sugar knows you.

This is not too hot for you to handle.

All the Ways to Get Clean

Seven

In the bath.

Through the thin walls she can hear her parents shouting at each other, but the running tap muffles the words, so she doesn't know what they're shouting about. This time.

If kids in school are yelling in the yard, the teachers rush out saying 'no fighting, no fighting' and hustle them all back to the classroom, everyone complaining they're missing break.
There's no-one to do that here, though.

The bath is full, so she shuts off the taps and lies back into the water, letting it lap into her ears, shutting out all the sounds except the steady thump of her heart and the pulse of the water in her ears, like the sea, that one time they went.

Seventeen

In the shower.

Should she take a shower? Should she think about last night? Do
something?

Talk to someone?

Her head hurts and she can't remember, just can't remember the details,
like in a dream.

There were people, drinks, more drinks, and she remembers kissing
him, wanting to do that.

But she can't join the dots between then and now.

So maybe she shouldn't be showering, but here she is, under scalding
water, scouring away the past, because if she's showering, then nothing
bad happened; nothing bad happened, did it?

Twenty-seven

In the bath.

Candle blurring out of focus. Water slopping over, drip, drip, drip on the wet floor like rain.

But it can't be rain, she thinks. Not inside.

There is banging: a sound that could not be made by water.

She wants to turn away from it, get free, but she's sliding underwater, and her hair floats out, and the noise is getting louder, and then finally something crashes through and she's thrashing and gasping and flailing, a newborn fish drowning in air and then...

... nothing, nothing, nothing...

... until her eyes open again and there's tubes and wires and noise and life.

Thirty-seven

In the shower.

Curled up in the tray with the hot then warm then cool water flowing over her like a blessing, hammering away at the pain in her head. The water beats down on her and she will beat this, she will beat it, she will beat it.

She has made a life worth living. Slowly, and with so much help. She will not let it slip away; she will live it.

When she's able to stay inside her skin without needing to peel it off.

The drumming water helps.

Now

In the bath.

Awkwardly washing the tiny body.

Reaching out for that third arm she would need to hold and wash and dry and towel-drape this tiny person who squeals at contact with the alien liquid, but slowly relaxes –

into the water,

into the love,

into her mother's arms.

Written In Ink

Mother always kept me concealed, and even in summer I had to wear a long, dark shirt; dark, to cover me so no-one would see. Mother would say that my skin burned easily, the lie she made, over-riding me so often if I began upon the truth, that her version became the fact and tumbled out effortlessly in its place. Every time we had to move on, I would tell this truth over and over to new, concerned faces.

Truth is, I was born with a tattoo. Though doctors disagreed, Mother assured me it was true. She had one just like it scrolling up her leg, while mine curves around one shoulder blade and down the middle of my spine. For the longest time, I could see it only in a mirror, squinting over my shoulder at its detail, backwards. It was not the kind of thing to photograph.

As I got older, I changed my truth. Long summer nights were spent drinking in the backs of cars by the river, or the lake, or the shore, stripping down to skinny dip in freezing water, feeling fingers trace their way gently, or roughly over me, showing my inner self to that part of the world drinking long and late and lazy by the water. Those days left tattoos of their own.

And always, we were flitting, stealing away. It's time to stopand settle, now I'm soon to be a mother too. If the ink has run through my veins and into hers, and she is born with her own tattoo, I vow not to hide it. I will show it to the sun; I will let the air and water in, to wash away our shame. Our shame that's written in ink.

Leaving Home

The heart rate of a mouse varies between 310 and 840 beats per minute. The respiratory rate is 80-230 breaths per minute. The body temperature is in a similar range to humans.

My mother is a mouse. Her whiskers twitch at loud noises, loud voices. Her pale grey fur stands to attention. I can feel her tiny heart, beating frantically against the soft walls of her ribcage. She knows the cat is nearby, senses it, smells it. But she is on her own mission. She straightens her tail, steps boldly away from the crack in the wall, makes herself known.

The normal heart rate of a cat is 140 to 220 beats per minute. Cats have a higher body temperature than humans.

My grandmother is a cat – righteous, green eyes locked unsparingly on her targets, licking cream and blood from her paws after each kill. Mostly, it's my mother who dies – a little more each time. There is a young bird on the lawn. Not a chick, with pale, fluffy down. An adult bird, with cream and brown-marked feathers, darkening at the tip, and a bright-rust tail. The cat watches steadily, moves silently. A rustle, nearby, makes its head turn quickly. The faint tinkling of a bell warns the bird into the air.

The resting heart rate of the red-tailed hawk is approx. 200 beats per minute. It has a temperature of 41C.

I am a hawk, and from where I sit on the air-currents, I can see the cat and mouse below me. When I was down there with them, I was a tug of war. I could feel the force of bothbut I did not like that pulling, tearing sensation. Now, they occupy themselves with each other, fur on fur, and I take to my feathers, and get clear. I fly, further and further away until the two creatures dwindle to tiny specks a long, long way down. I feel the warmth of the sun on my feathers and I soar, ever further, ever closer, ever away.

A Temporal Haunting

I catch a glimpse of her, at least I think it's her. Just something nudging at the corner of my eye as I run errands. I threw on gym clothes and trainers this morning, promising my slightly oily roots a shower after the school run, after I've picked up the kitchen, before lunch definitely, but here I am, buying groceries mid-afternoon, no shower. It's her hair that snags my attention. It looks expensive. It looks like time and money. Money and time, time and money. Two things I don't have enough of. I remember that hair. I had that hair, once.

'Do you smell flowers?' I ask the kids, distracting them from homework, ask Dan, who taffy-pulls his head up from his phone. Blank faces. I'm the only one who catches a familiar whiff of ambered jasmine. My nose twitches on molecules of sherbet scent. She's been here, bringing that perfumed past with her. I used to spray my wrists, my pulsing throat, with that exact mix. So long ago. In the time before time. Before kids. Before marriage, or maybe overlapping those early, loved-up years. What I want to know now is how she got in.

The days I'm not working from home are the worst. Dan showers, drinks a solitary coffee, takes the early train before the kids wake up. I wrangle, and wrangle – school uniforms, brushing teeth, breakfasts and packed lunches – promising my hair I'll wash it tonight; tonight I won't be too wiped by my day. I power, head down, through the commute, to my desk. She's everywhere, just beyond my peripheral vision. At the water cooler, taking time for a lunch break, fixing her perfect makeup. I drag my attention back to my work and try to clamp down time, stop it from speeding past too quickly. I never have enough to spend it on a whim. I don't have time to look for her. I don't want to see her.

Wednesdays I have to get home early to take the kids to their swimming lessons. I sit in the chlorine-scented humid fug poolside, answering emails on my phone, one eye on the pool, on the bobbing heads, identical in their swim hats. 'Yes, darling, I saw you, you were great,' I'll be able to say later. Almost truthfully. Is that her, swiping her membership card at the desk? Changing from one sleek suit to another, her taut body diving into the adult pool? I don't have the resources to look. The steaming heat of the pool makes my clothes too close, too tight. I want to fling them off and dive in myself, like I used to, after work, so many years ago. But I have emails, and small humans to cheer on, so that's what I do.

Dan says we don't have fun anymore. What I hear is that I'm no fun anymore, though he denies this interpretation. I wrangle the kids, go to work, wrangle homework and dinner, then doze through an hour of Netflix or Prime, willing myself off the sofa to go take that shower. Fun is time I don't have. But he talks about getting out for the night, just the two of us, getting my parents over to watch the kids, or a sitter. I hear her bell-like laugh, clear and sweet, like the tinkle of champagne bubbles in a glass, and I say 'sure' and 'let's do it' and 'book it', like I have the energy for this.

The regular sitter isn't available. Somehow, she's grown up and gone to college since we last called, so my parents are coming over for the night. We found the spare room – under the layers of laundry, and old toys, last winter's clothes waiting to be put away – and cleaned it out, vacuuming and changing sheets. I ran to the shops for mom's favourite wine and dad's favourite beers. I thought I saw her walking past me, to the pretty little beauty salon I must try, as I loaded the car with groceries to make a nice dinner for my parents, and to have a good brunch for before they head home again tomorrow. I thought I saw her, but my new glasses slipped down my sweaty nose, so I can't be sure.

We make our dinner reservation, just. I've already made dinner, while the kids whooped and shrieked around the house, delighted with visitors. I had my shower. It's good my hair is short now. It's almost dry. There was a moment, sitting on the edge of the bed when I thought of just lying back, and closing my eyes. But now I'm here, a glass of wine in my hand and I definitely see her reflected in the deep plate glass windows here. She's at my table, and she looks so young, and fun. She's the kind of woman who'll end the night dancing in a club, mascara still perfect. Pretty. Happy. Like it's twenty years ago. I think Dan sees her too. And then I slide my glasses on again and she's gone. It's just me, and Dan. I slip my glasses off again and raise my glass to her. 'Who are you toasting?' Dan asks, turning round to scan the busy restaurant. 'Just us,' I say, 'just us. And the future.'

Fiona McKay is a SmokeLong Quarterly Emerging Writer Fellow for 2023. Writes with Writers'HQ. Words now or forthcoming in *Bath Flash, Lumiere Review, Janus Literary, Pithead Chapel, The Forge* and others. Runner-up in Bath Novella-in-Flash 2023. Her writing has been nominated for Best Microfictions and Best Small Fictions. Her Novella-in-Flash, The Top Road, is forthcoming with AdHoc Fiction. She is supported by the Arts Council Ireland Agility Award and lives beside the sea in Dublin, Ireland, with her husband and daughter.

Tweets about writing @fionaemckayryan

Acknowledgements

This Flash Collection contains pieces from 2021-2023 and I have so many people to thank for their support and friendship during this time.

Half of the stories in this collection come from Writers'HQ Flash Face Off – so this is a huge thank you to everyone on the forum who has liked or commented on my pieces. And to Kathy Hoyle – whose WHQ Flash Fiction course started my Flash Fiction writing – for all her encouragement. There is a huge gang of wonderful people who take part in FFO and any list can only represent some of them, so thank you to everyone I've met there over the past two years, and in particular Rachel, Audrey, Tavia, Michelle, Julia, Dot, Joyce, Paula, Sumitra, Heather, Jo, JP, Sarah, Maria, Mark, Mark, Duncan, Claire, Kirsti, Mat, Jim, Terry, Sarah, Clodagh, Kate, Mazz, and everyone else who writes, reads, and comments. I hope you all know what a fantastic group of people you are, and such great writers.

Five of the stories in the collection were written on various courses run by Matt Kendrick. I have learned so much about writing at sentence-level and word-level from Matt's courses – about rhythm and sound, about how to sharpen my images and use all the senses. Huge thanks, Matt, for your teaching, editing, and support.

Other stories in the collection were written in Retreat West's Friday Flashing, and Flash Fiction Festival's online festival days – both of these have been wonderful sources of inspiration over the last two years.

And finally, SmokeLong Fitness, where one of the stories started in the January Intensive this year with Elisabeth Ingram Wallace. SmokeLong Fitness is another wonderful source of inspiration and craft learning. Thank you to Christopher Allen, Helen Rye, and all the SmokeLong Team

Writing can be a solitary thing - writer-friends and writing groups are essential. I've been so lucky with both.

Firstly, I'd like to thank my best writer-pal, Rachel O'Cleary, who has been the most terrific support, first reader, and sounding board. And a constant inspiration with her fabulous writing!

I'm part of a critique group, and the support and friendship of the Flash Amigas – Slawka Scarso, Denise Bayes, Suzanne Green, Noémi Schierling-Olah, and Eleonora Balsano – has been just essential! We started out as writing-colleagues and have ended up as the very best of friends.

The very wonderful Sara Hills invited me to be part of a long-project support group she and Ali McGrane were putting together – and what started out as accountability ended up as wonderful friendship and support. Putting together this collection was one of the things I made myself accountable for, and thanks to all in the Cheer group for keeping me on task! Sara, together with Rosaleen Lynch, Ali McGrane, Slawka Scarso, Rachel O'Cleary – you are the best, and thank you so much!

Finally, but most importantly, I'd like to thank my husband, Declan, and my daughter, Jane, for their support – and the gift of time to write. Jane is a wonderful artist and created the cover art for this collection.

The author received financial support from the Arts Council Ireland in the creation of this work.

Publications

Some of the pieces in this collection were previously published, and I am grateful to each and every one of the following –

The Destroying Angel – *Free Flash Fiction – September 2022*
Ground Truth – *Sledgehammer Lit – August 2021*
The Magic Hour – *Funny Pearls – June 2021*
How to Paint a Masterpiece (In Seven Easy Steps) – *Cranked Anvil Flash Anthology – May 2021*
Grift – *Twin Pies Literary – Volume: The Gentle Slope*
Trust Fall – *Books Ireland Magazine – December 2022*
Afterlife – *EllipsisZine Ten – November 2021*
Visiting Time – *Five Minutes – August 2021 & One Wild Ride – April 2023*
A Recipe for Disaster – *The Birdseed – December 2021 – Nominated for Best Microfiction*
A Temporal Haunting – *Ellipsis – January 2023*

Printed in Great Britain
by Amazon

44566717R00066